WITHDRAWN

A Note to Parents and Caregivers:

Read-it! Readers are for children who are just starting on the amazing road to reading. These beautiful books support both the acquisition of reading skills and the love of books.

 The PURPLE LEVEL presents basic topics and objects using high frequency words and simple language patterns.

 The RED LEVEL presents familiar topics using common words and repeating sentence patterns.

 The BLUE LEVEL presents new ideas using a larger vocabulary and varied sentence structure.

 The YELLOW LEVEL presents more challenging ideas, a broad vocabulary, and wide variety in sentence structure.

 The GREEN LEVEL presents more complex ideas, an extended vocabulary range, and expanded language structures.

 The ORANGE LEVEL presents a wide range of ideas and concepts using challenging vocabulary and complex language structures.

When sharing a book with your child, read in short stretches, pausing often to talk about the pictures. Have your child turn the pages and point to the pictures and familiar words. And be sure to reread favorite stories or parts of stories.

There is no right or wrong way to share books with children. Find time to read with your child, and pass on the legacy of literacy.

Adria F. Klein, Ph.D.
Professor Emeritus
California State University
San Bernardino, California

Editor: Jill Kalz
Page Production: Jaime Martens
Creative Director: Keith Griffin
Editorial Director: Carol Jones
Managing Editor: Catherine Neitge
The illustrations in this book were created digitally.

Picture Window Books
5115 Excelsior Boulevard
Suite 232
Minneapolis, MN 55416
877-845-8392
www.picturewindowbooks.com

Printed in the United States of America.

Library of Congress Cataloging-in-Publication Data
Jones, Christianne C.
Camping trip / by Christianne C. Jones ; illustrated by James Demski, Jr.
p. cm. — (Read-it! readers)
Summary: Mike is always clumsy and inept when he goes camping with his friends,
but one night his problems come in handy.
ISBN 1-4048-1167-2 (hardcover)
[1. Camping—Fiction.] I. Demski, James, 1976– ill. II. Title. III. Series.

PZ7.J6823Cam 2005
[E]—dc22
                                                        2005003856

Camping Trip

by Christianne C. Jones
illustrated by James Demski Jr.

Special thanks to our advisers for their expertise:

Adria F. Klein, Ph.D.
Professor Emeritus, California State University
San Bernardino, California

Susan Kesselring, M.A.
Literacy Educator
Rosemount–Apple Valley–Eagan (Minnesota) School District

PiCTURE WiNDOW BOOKS
Minneapolis, Minnesota

Bob, Jane, Brian, and Mike went camping every summer.

And every summer, Mike had a lot of problems.

Bob set up the tents.

6

Mike tripped over the ropes.

Jane sprayed for bugs.

Mike got bit.

Brian collected sticks.

Mike ran into a tree.

Bob built a fire.

Mike put it out.

Jane cooked supper.

Mike dropped his food.

Brian went fishing.

Mike fell in.

Bob, Jane, and Brian went to sleep.

Mike stayed up.

19

One night, Mike heard a strange noise behind the tent. A bear was digging through the trash!

20

Mike screamed. Bob, Jane, and Brian
woke up.

The scared bear ran away.

Mike saved the day.

More *Read-it!* Readers

Bright pictures and fun stories help you practice your reading skills. Look for more books at your level.

Back to School by Christianne C. Jones

Bamboo at Jungle School by Lucie Papineau

The Best Snowman by Margaret Nash

Bill's Baggy Pants by Susan Gates

Cleo and Leo by Anne Cassidy

Fable's Whistle by Michael Dahl

Felix on the Move by Maeve Friel

I Am in Charge of Me by Dana Meachen Rau

Jasper and Jess by Anne Cassidy

The Lazy Scarecrow by Jillian Powell

Let's Share by Dana Meachen Rau

Little Joe's Big Race by Andy Blackford

The Little Star by Deborah Nash

Meg Takes a Walk by Susan Blackaby

The Naughty Puppy by Jillian Powell

Selfish Sophie by Damian Kelleher

The Tall, Tall Slide by Michael Dahl

Looking for a specific title or level? A complete list of *Read-it!* Readers is available on our Web site:
www.picturewindowbooks.com